FAMILY CIRCUS®

QUIET, SAM!

Bil Keane

THE FAMILY CIRCUS
©1990 Bil Keane, Inc.
Distributed Worldwide by
King Features Syndicate, Inc.

A Fawcett Gold Medal Book
Published by Ballantine Books
Copyright © 1990 by Bil Keane, Inc.
Distributed by King Features Syndicate, Inc.

ISBN 0-449-14616-2

Manufactured in the United States of America

First Ballantine Books Edition: August 1990

"Some dogs bark, little dogs yap,
and big dogs woof."

"Listen! I hear a buzz-keeto"

"When dogs are happy they don't have to bother smiling. They just wag their tails."

"Mommy, are you gonna need a few
eggs opened up today?"

"Thanks a lot, you guys. If it
wasn't for you I could have
had a hamster."

"Grandma has a neat phone, Mommy!
You put your fingers in holes
and spin this wheel!"

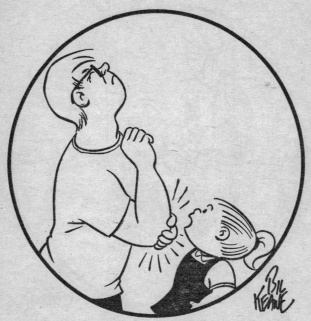

"Aren't you s'posed to laugh when you
bump your funny bone?"

"Very good! Now spell 'dog' . . . Right!
How about 'cat?' . . . good boy!
Now spell. . . ."

"Mommy will you take this weed out
of this strawberry?"

"Are there ever any BOY poodles?"

"Daddy does the giant better."

"The more you hear the better
we sound."

"I think we're in trouble. Mommy just
called for William and Jeffrey."

"How do angels get their nightshirts
on over their wings?"

"He stabbed her to make her stop singing."

"You've drawn a nice birthday card, Billy,
but I think Mommy will like it better
if you didn't put her age on it."

". . . and we're all takin' you out to Peter
Piper Pizza for dinner as soon as you
get us ready!"

"I don't like drums. They don't have
enough notes."

"Instead of sayin' I had an 'upset tummy,'
couldn't you say 'belly ache?' "

"That's Mars. It's named after a
candy bar."

"But the guy on the radio said spring
begins today."

"Mommy! I LIKE it when somebody
says I look older."

"PJ can reach the bathroom lock now!"

"Would you eat the top of my yogurt, Mommy? The fruit is at the bottom."

"Some man called to tell us he's
got the wrong number."

"Why didn't Chicken Little check
her news sources?"

"I won't kick you again, Mommy."

"I'm not asking for anything in particular,
but you could surprise me."

"How do Easter lilies know what date
they hafta have flowers?"

"The Easter Bunny really knows how to count. He gave us each the same number of jelly beans."

"Mommy! There's an April Foo . . . I mean,
there's an alligator in the bathtub!"

"I think PJ caught what Barfy had. His nose is warm."

"Hard-boiled eggs can be any color,
but scrambled eggs hafta
be yellow."

"Put YOUR hair in a ponytail, Mommy,
so we can be twins."

"Looks like winter's gone into extra innings."

"Daddy, Mommy wants to talk to you
whenever you wake up."

"Is that all a comet does?"

"Mustn't touch knives, P.J. They're all
rated PG13."

"SWEET dreams? Aren't they bad
for my teeth?"

"I need a 'brella, Mommy. It's starting to dribble."

"I don't remember how hard I studied,
but I know I gave it my best shot."

"Stop wastin' wood, Billy. It doesn't
grow on trees, y'know."

"Those are all the snails I collected
at recess last Friday."

"Why didn't they give a girl's name
to Little Bo Pete?"

"The windshield wipers remind me of
Barfy's tail."

"The only naughty words we can use
in this house are 'darn,'
'heck' and 'dickens.' "

"Kittycat just rearranged her nap."

"Daddy's tucking in the car."

"My Mom sent my cute sayings to Reader's Digest, but they didn't want any of them."

"It's only raining kittens and puppies."

"If you don't clean your room I'll trade you."

"God likes girls best. That's why he didn't give us whiskers."

"I was hidin' but nobody would go
seek me."

"Daddy watches anything that has at least two people and a ball in it."

"That bird did a pretty good job building
a nest with no hands, just his mouth."

"At school we don't have potties. We
have laboratories."

"Can I keep this dollar I found in your
purse, Mommy?"

"May is my favorite month. It's the
easiest one to spell."

"Did you see the feathers out there,
Daddy? That's why we're not
speakin' to Kittycat!"

"How old do I have to be to have a
Sweet Sixteen party?"

"Somebody let me know
when PJ spills his milk."

"Yeeulk! It's a STUNK!"

"How many times
have I told you
not to do that?"

"Three?"

"I forget. What am I givin' him?"

"It's not scribbling! It's DOODLIN'!"

"Poor Mommy. We get to go to the
movies for Mother's Day and
she has to stay home."

"I'm lonesome for a chocolate
chip cookie."

"Mommy! This bush is havin'
a flower!"

"Old people get bent over so they can look
at their grandchildren."

"Look what I found. A leaf
from a bird!"

"I was just kiddin', PJ. Sharks
can only go in salt water!"

"Very good! NOW draw a robot with a
beard riding a horse watching
Halley's Comet."

"Would you tell Jeffy to stop his
tummy from gargling?"

"Don't discourage him. Do you
know how much carpenters
are earning now?"

"I think I flunked the transformer test.
I couldn't make robots out of a
dinosaur or a grasshopper."

"Daddy! There's a funny new show
on called 'Leave it to Beaver'!"

"We're making mud quiches."

"Why does 'Morial Day make your
eyes watery, Grandma?"

"PJ picked a flower that's only
half done."

"I'm too sleepy to go to bed."

"What did I tell you children about
slamming that..."

"I like the way they tee up
these dandelions."

"Look! Grandma used to hang
clothes on a jumpin' rope."

"I really don't care about a moment
of silence in school, but I'd like to
have one here occasionally."

"I don't like yawning that long."

"You don't have to press down so hard."
"But I really MEAN what I'm writing!"

"Pigs all look like they've got their
faces against windows."

"You'll never grow up to be President
'cause people won't vote for somebody who can't tie his shoelaces."

"If Chris McCauley's mother lets him jump off a cliff, would you want me to let you do it, too?"

"Don't ask me how they get IN the eggs.
All I know is they get out of them."

"This bulb is empty."

"Don't plant anything in fair
territory, Mommy."

"Poor Daddy. When he was little
they didn't have cable TV."

"Is that a camouflage shirt for
fighting in flower gardens?"

"Climate — C-L-I-M... uh — I'd like
to buy a vowel, please?"

"That's a face only a mother could love, Jeffy, and I'm NOT your mother."

"A little to the left — now down just a
bit — ahhhh! THERE!"

"But outside there's no rugs to
catch us!"

"How come girl cats have
whiskers, too?"

"Why do they have a lifeguard?"

"Get up, Billy! You're
wastin' vacation!"

"I found a SIX-leaf clover
with two stems!"

"Daddy doesn't eat bacon and eggs
'cause he's cutting down on his
lester oil."

"Look how long Barfy gets in
the summer."

"The answer to that one is 'World War II.'"
"No, Daddy. On the card it says
'World War Eleven.'"

"Mommy! Look at the big pickles!"

"Butterflies are smarter than Frisbees."

"Aw, Mommy! You couldn't REALLY grow potatoes in my ears, could you?"

"Would you come out for a while, Mommy?
We're havin' a parade and we need
somebody to watch."

"She shouldn't hold it up so high,
'cause so many people arrive on
airplanes now."

"Mommy! We need more hands!"

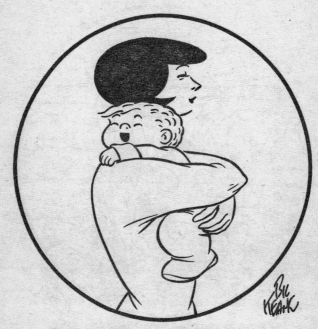

"This is my favorite place —
inside your hug."

"They were lucky in the old days.
Their bathrooms were right out
in the backyard."

"Which is it, Mommy — don't RUN or
don't TALK with a lollipop in
your mouth?"

"When I ask you which hand it's in
don't guess this one."

"You have an answer for everything,
don't you?... Don't you?..."

"I'm glad baseball doesn't have a net."

"When 'All My Children' comes on all
MOMMY'S children hafta go outside."

"Settle it yourselves! I am NOT a referee!"

"Jeffy's being disgussin' again."

"Satellite dishes look like knocked-over beach umbrellas."

"Every time I go to catch a lightning bug,
he turns his light off."

"In the army they have these hard things
you hafta do called optical courses."

"After I take one more bite of my dinner, THEN can I have a peanut butter and jelly sandwich?"

"REAL friends don't hafta keep talking
all the time."